CAN YOU LIVE

AFTER THE FIRE

by TARA REEVES

For information regarding special discounts or bulk purchases, please
contact Tara Reeves at tarareeves730@gmail.com; Facebook: Tara
Reeves; YouTube: iLivefitb....Tara Reeves

ISBN: 978-0-9991590-1-9

Library of Congress Control Number: In publication data

Can You Live After the FIRE
Author: Tara Reeves
Cover Design: MagicMike
Editor: Jennyhills247
Published by: iLIVE Publishing Compny

Acknowledgments

I will not start without first giving
Honor to God for all He has done.

I have done a lot. I've been through a lot
and God brought me through it all.

I would like to thank my sons:
Nikkida, Malik, Mikhail and *Najee.*

These young men have been the very being of my focus and
motivation to pursue the dreams and goals for my family.

I love you all and bless God for all the things we have
gone through and came out together in Victory!

To my *Mom, Joan Garden,* you are the sunshine of my life and
the Wind beneath my Wings. I have not met anyone in my life
that is stronger than you. To have been through so much and
still love God, life, people and self, is absolutely amazing.

I have no excuse to give up because when I look
at you all excuses go out through the window.

So you know, I am telling you, Joan Garden, I love you!

To my *Dad, Bernard Dupree Reeves*, I will
always love you and I miss you every day.

Thank you for being the fire under me,
always telling me that I can do more.

To all my Grandparents, Brothers, Sisters, Aunts, Uncles,
Cousins, Nieces, Nephews and Friends THANK YOU!

I have to say to ALL OF THE PASTORS, EVANGELISTS,
INTERCESSORS, PRAYER WARRIORS, AND PEOPLE OF
GOD WHO SPOKE, PRAYED, BELIEVED AND AGREED
WITH ME – THANK YOU AND GOD BLESS YOU ALL!
XOXOX

Dedication

I *dedicate* THIS book to EVERYONE
GOING THROUGH THE FIRE!

Wherever you are in THIS process of
your journey, I *dedicate* this book to You!

I *dedicate* this book to you for your Courage to F-ight.

I *dedicate* this to you for your Strength that is I-mmeasurable.

I *dedicate* this to you for your Faith to R-ecover.

I *dedicate* this book to YOU when you
E-merge. OUT OF THE *FIRE!*

What's in the Book?

To the Readers

As you hold this book in your hand, you may be wondering... *Why did she write this book? What is this book actually about?*

"Why write a book?" You may ask.

"What's THIS book going to be about?" You may question.

I sat and thought about the best way to answer these questions without being fake and deep.

I wanted to answer with a different attitude.

All that came to mind was this..."If anything that I went through in MY life whether positive or negative can help someone through their life seasons, then that's the reason for this book. "

THIS BOOK IS ABOUT LIFE!

One Day I'm Gonna Be…

I believe that every child in the world that enters kindergarten is asked the same question. "What do you want to be when you grow up?"

Most answers consist of careers like doctors, lawyers, firefighters, nurses, and teachers. That's what they would like to believe anyway.

Who would dare argue with a five-year-old to say, "No, you're not! You're going to be a high school dropout, a drug addict, homeless, or a domestic abuse victim."

Who would not want the best for their children?

Most parents want more for their children than what they had in their own childhood. Now, whether that happens or not is entirely another story.

Many obstacles, traps, distractions and hindrances in a child's life can make reaching the goals set out by parents almost unobtainable.

Life has its own way of setting standards and limits that will alter where you can end up if you solely depend on the difficult times you might have experienced. But Thank God for *His* plans. Man Look! I cannot sit here and act as if I had this revelation from the beginning because that would definitely be a **bold-faced** lie!

Let's do an exercise to break the ice.

What did you want to be when you were growing up? Did you achieve them? Why or why not?

_____

_____

_____

_____

_____

_____

_____

_____

_____

_____

_____

_____

The Smoke Before the Fire

I had my own issues to deal with on a daily basis in the form of low self-esteem.

I am my mother's middle child and my father's first born. They divorced when I was very young.

My father was a shell-shocked, alcoholic Vietnam veteran. So there were different disadvantages between my siblings and I.

We had different fathers but my stepfather sent me to a Catholic school for my elementary years since my sister needed to be walked to school for kindergarten.

I guess it would not have been morally right to send her to a private school and me to a public school, especially when we were close in age. When my mother and stepfather divorced, I ended up going to a public school while my sister went on to a private school because her father paid for it.

Public school for me brought on an onslaught of challenges, hurt and heart aches which added on to the issues already in my life.

That desire wanting to be a part of the "in crowd" and not being able to fit in because I didn't have the right clothes, hair do, and associates was the worse for a teenager who already felt like a misfit.

I had stuff to deal with that I wanted to ignore so that I could function as "normal" as possible, but I had bones in my bag that I tried to bury while trying to be safe in my own world.

My mom did what she could then being a single parent, working and still trying to have a life of her own.

She was a very strong mother who did not play any games when it had to do with my siblings and myself. She didn't accept any stories of why we couldn't do what was required from us in school. She believed that you could do whatever you put your mind to do.

I guess with her raising my disabled brother from a young age, there was no room for any doubt in her will to do.

She did whatever it took to make sure my brother had the education, training, medical attention, and respect that all others had in those times.

There wasn't a lot of help for her but she made it. People didn't make it easy at all for her but she still made it; so her STANDARDS for us were high.

I had to guard myself from the men introduced to us as her new boyfriends or "uncles." They seemed like the nicest people until I saw and experienced that they had another agenda which was me.

I woke up to one standing over me, pulling up my nightgown because I slept with no underwear at age 11–12. There was another incident where he made the statement, "if you keep sleeping with your butt in the air like that, I might have to put something in there." What do you do with this kind of action? I did what I thought was the right thing by telling my mom about it.

I have to say that was the hardest thing to do because the tongue lashing and disbelief I received was shocking.

So, I experienced these kinds of actions from her boyfriends until I left home at sixteen.

I was in and out of relationships from fourteen when I lost my virginity to a nineteen-year-old to meeting people on the chat line, then meeting them in the middle of the night in Prices Park.

I went from going to church every Sunday, Wednesday and any other time the doors were opened to running the streets, being promiscuous and uncontrollable.

So, when I got to the point that, "I wanted to be grown or smell myself," as they say, my mom gave me a choice to follow her rules or get out.

I had such a longing and void to be loved that I was trying to find it ANYWHERE with ANYONE!

Think about how you were raised. Do you think it affected your current life decisions?

_____

_____

_____

_____

_____

_____

_____

_____

_____

_____

_____

Where There's Smoke There's Fire

This was the beginning of an ENORMOUS FIRE!

The very things seen in everyone else's life, which were happiness, success, and love, I wanted in my own life.

Love to me had been such a distant goal or a never-ending fantasy. I really wanted to be loved by any means necessary.

Whatever form "love" presented itself opened me up to things that I definitely was not ready for.

So, here comes this opportunity for me to babysit for one of my family members "male friends" who had two boys.

I thought he was a handsome guy. He seemed fun to be around when I played with his boys.

One night when he picked the boys up, he told me that he had always wanted to kiss me and asked if I would let him kiss me.

The idea of being kissed by an older man was intriguing. So I let him kiss me; and that was the open door that I told you I was not ready for.

It was from that point on we started secretly dating.

We both knew my mom would hit the ceiling if she ever found out about us dating. So I would lie about babysitting so that we could go to a motel, a park, a car or wherever to have sex.

The time spent together did not go unnoticed and my mother was informed about it.

She did her own investigation and found us at a local motel one night.

She had him locked up and tried to press charges for statutory rape. But because I would not say anything the cops could not do anything.

That was when she gave me the option of following her rules or leaving.

I decided I was going to leave and be with my boyfriend, who was fifteen years older than me. I was sixteen and he was thirty one.

I moved into his sister's house with him, his two children, his sister and brother. It was a three bedroom house but the children, he and I stayed in one bedroom.

It was good for the first couple of days, but by the next week his sister was making it very clear that she did not want me there.

She was telling him that she did not want an underaged girl, who was still in school, living in her house with a grown man. I think her concern was that she worked with the State and it could affect her job if anyone found out.

I had to endure the brother who was absolutely disturbed, and a pervert.

The kids were a handful and had issues and my boyfriend was not all I thought he would be.

He didn't work; he barely took care of the kids, and he was a very mean man.

The thing that blew my mind was that you really don't know people until you live with them.

So, for me, I was confused to find out that the man that seemed so nice in the beginning was a monster or a wolf in sheep's clothing.

He started with the little subtle things like getting upset because I was talking to a guy at work.

I didn't think anything of it. I actually thought it was cute that he was being protective over me.

Then the little comments like, "I don't want you running around with those so-called friends of yours because most of them aren't in a relationship."

"They're jealous of what you got. So they're going to do anything to break us up."

This was how he started isolating me to the point that my friends eventually stopped coming by and calling me.

My problem has been trying to save the people who didn't want to save themselves from self-destruction.

I took the bullets, hits, stabs, and other attacks trying to save people who didn't want to save themselves. I had taken care and protected people all my childhood and adult life so much that when I tried to focus on myself it seemed wrong.

My mom didn't talk to me that much anymore when I moved in with my boyfriend. I saw my sister in passing like when she was on her way to school or going to the corner store.

My routine was go to school, pick up the kids from daycare, go home and sit in the prison which was our room.

I had always been an outgoing person but when I got in the relationship with him, all of that changed.

I literally sat by the window and watched my days go by.

Now here are some questions.

Can you think of a time when you felt alone or trapped? How did that make you feel? What were some of the thoughts that went through your head?

_____

_____

_____

_____

_____

_____

_____

_____

_____

_____

_____

Fire Starter

I received a call from my best friend, Tracy, one day and we talked like we usually did about everything when I heard him calling me. So we said our good-byes.

I got off the phone, walked up to the bedroom door and got slapped so hard that I thought I had seen stars, all because he heard me say a man's name in conversation with my best friend.

That day came that every woman has talked about with their girlfriends about what their REACTION would be if it ever happened to them.

My first reaction was, "Oh my God! Did he just hit me?" It became very clear that he did because he was standing right over of me yelling.

I believe I was in shock or so scared that I don't remember anything he had said to me.

He explained that he didn't mean to hit me but it made him mad that I was talking about another man. He declared he would never do it again.

Now I know that I am supposed to ask the questions at the end. But some things need to be asked right when you feel it.

If you are in an ABUSIVE RELATIONSHIP of ANY KIND (man or woman), please reach out for help! Child Inc 302-762-6110 or 911 or email me tarareeves730@gmail.com *so we can figure this out together! YOU ARE NOT ALONE!*

WHEN the first hit happened, how did you feel? What did you do? What were you thinking?

_____

_____

_____

_____

_____

_____

_____

_____

_____

His way of making up with me was by having sex, but in my mind I was being raped.

Ironically, I had been through a rape experience before but this day I can say that I CONSCIOUSLY knew *that my life had changed completely.*

The abuse went from pushing, to slaps, then escalated to strangling and punching.

It was days that I could tell that he was in one of those moods and I was going to be beaten and it didn't matter if the kids were in the room or if his sister was home.

I remember burning food and he started hollering, cursing and slapping me to the point that his sister tried to help me.

She told him that if he could not get himself together, then he would have to get out of her house. She told me that I needed to go back home to my mom but, because I was young, stupid, and supposedly in love, her suggestions went in through one ear and out the other.

Now that his sister was involved with how he treated me, he decided that we should get our own place. I knew he was going to do whatever it took to get the money for us to move.

I just did what I was told and tried to stay out of everybody's way.

His sister still was irritating me and I ignored her as much as possible until the day I had enough. It started as an argument and ended in a fight.

The kids were right there and she didn't know that I was pregnant when she fell on top of me, causing me to miscarry. His reply was, "why were you fighting my sister?" I didn't want to explain. So I just hung up.

I got to the hospital where they performed an ultrasound and the report was a spontaneous abortion or a miscarriage that was devastating news.

The next couple of weeks I was depressed, confused, and angry.

I was trying to understand why all of this was happening to me and how I could get out of this or if I was going to get out of this alive.

My mom saw the scratches on my face and wanted to know what had happened.

I had to tell her because if she had asked them herself, it would have definitely been a fight. I told her I had it under control so she wouldn't worry about me or worse still, tell my family. I came to the realization that she did love me but she had to let me go if I couldn't obey and respect her rules.

Have you ever looked back on a decision you made to defy a parent and it was not only wrong but detrimental? Why?

_____

_____

_____

_____

_____

_____

_____

_____

_____

_____

_____

I ended up getting pregnant again about a good month after the miscarriage.

I still was going to school just for pregnant teenagers with my sister and cousin. I was a few weeks from getting my diploma when I went into labor January 24 around 2:30 am.

I called the ambulance. When they arrived my mom saw the lights and came outside only to see me on my way to the hospital. She met us there.

I did not know the amount of pain having a child could cause but when I say, "OH MY GOD!" that's the way my body felt. They had to coach me to open my legs so the baby could come out. He was born with a long head from being stuck in the birthing canal.

It wasn't long after Nikkida was born that we moved into an apartment on 9th Jefferson. I believe he wanted to get me away from my family and friends and ultimately into his complete grips. April of 1989, the very thing for which I had called so many people stupid was the very thing that HE introduced to me.

DRUGS: HEROIN, COCAINE, and CRACK (Bundles)!

He called me into the bathroom while he was preparing the needle the coke and heroin, and he posed this question-

"Do you love me?" I answered, "Of course I do."

He gestured me to come and sit down and went on to explain to me that he wanted me to experience what he was doing when he got high. He went on to say that it was my way to show him how much I loved and trusted him if I let him shoot me up with heroin and cocaine.

What happened next? I don't know. I remember standing in the hallway and it began to stretch like in the movies!!!! waaaaayyyyyyyyy doooowwwnnn tttthhhheeerrrrreeeee!!!! and I fell out! I woke up in the shower.

We got high on every weekend and the 1st of the month was party night! Then it went to every time we had money or when we could hustle up money.

I was introduced to all kinds of people who would come over and get high. I was taken to places in Philadelphia and Chester, in the projects and down nasty halls to apartments that looked like something off of TV.

I now look back and just tell God – thank you for YOUR protection.

RIGHT HERE IS YOUR PRAISE BREAK.............

We met a white couple underneath us who wanted me to babysit, but he definitely was not having that especially after inviting us down for drinks and tried to introduce me to LSD. I was trying my best to take care of the three boys 5,4 and 4 months.

I did the best I could with the children and getting high until one night the baby stopped breathing. I *ran* to the hospital with him wrapped in a blanket and I called my mom once I got there.

I stayed there at the hospital with my son and the nurse informed me that they needed to take an x ray of my sons' chest and asked if I was pregnant I jokingly answered, "I didn't know."

She asked if I wanted to take a pregnancy test and I said sure why not and that is how I found out that I was pregnant with my second son.

I truly believe that was the cause of his autism because I was getting high and didn't even know I was 2 months pregnant.

Malik did not have difficulties at birth but as time went on we could definitely see that there was something different and unique about him.

During the third pregnancy I didn't get high at all. I guess I felt guilty about getting high and not even noticing the changes in my body indicating that I was pregnant. Mikhail's birth was difficult because he didn't want to come out. So I had to push him out at 8 cm. My fourth pregnancy with Najee, their dad talked me into smoking crack when I was about 7 months. I got high for a couple of weeks but I stopped when he stopped moving.

I confided in my counselor and she told me all the risks associated with getting high and that information gave me enough conviction not to continue get high WHILE I was pregnant.*One thing I can say is that I was very honest with my sons about my past because I would rather have them hear it from me than someone on the street.*

Now this is a hard question...Is there anything about your past that your children or parent(s) would be hurt, shocked, embarrassed or betrayed if they heard it from someone other than you?

_____

_____

_____

_____

_____

_____

_____

_____

_____

_____

_____

Do you think you would ever tell them? Why or why not?

_____

_____

_____

_____

_____

_____

_____

_____

_____

_____

_____

I continued getting high after the boys were born. I wanted to stop but with their dad doing it, supplying it and literally giving it to me, it was not easy to stop.

I remember one time when my youngest son was a few weeks

old. I was getting high when my chest started getting tight and pain was rushing through my heart.

I started getting short of breath and the room started spinning.

I felt like I was dying slowly.

No one paid any attention when I grabbed my chest, jumped up and walked away from the table. All I could do was go into my infant son's room and cry, "please God don't let me die like this!" I sat on the floor crying with my son in my arms.

Thank God He answered that prayer and now here I am writing this book.

Later, I was talking to my aunt about the situation, she told me that she was awaken out of her sleep with chest pains and just started praying for whoever was in some kind of trouble, not knowing that she was actually feeling and praying for me.

The Bible says, *"The effectual fervent prayer of a righteous man availeth much" (James 5:16).*

So I have to be so grateful that God heard and answered someone's prayer for me.

You never know how much it means to have people in your life that have a relationship with God until serious situations or circumstances present themselves.

Go back to a time that you KNOW that someone was praying for you and God answered them.

_____

_____

_____

_____

_____

_____

_____

_____

_____

This madness of drugs and abusive relationship lasted from 1986 until August 13, 1993.

Why do I remember the date?

My answer to that question is simply this: "That was the day the Lord visited me!"

He came to me in a dream and asked me, **"What do YOU want**

for YOUR life?"

The Lord showed me looking like a dry, brown, withering flower in a dark corner dying Then He showed me in a field of green grass, sunlight and I was in the middle of this beautiful meadow laughing, running and loving life.

What do I have to do to make you move? Do I have to take your first born?

What the Lord showed me was my first son being hit by a car because I was so high that I wasn't paying attention to him. Let me tell you that I got up that morning after getting high all night, grabbed my Bible, my journal, pampers, bottles and my babies and I called my friend, Kim and asked if she could come get me now before I changed my mind to get away from him. I felt like I could not move fast enough.

She literally was there in 10 minutes! That girl must have been on the corner!

I kissed my two step-sons (whom I wish I could have taken but their dad would have literally killed me) and left. I went to the battered women shelter and, as soon as I got in the door, I asked them to start my divorce papers.

Yeah, I married him with the proposal that I would never forget. His proposal was, "If you don't marry me, I'm going to beat you so bad that you will be in the hospital!" So how could a girl turn a proposal like that down? So we got married in our apartment with his long time drug buddy as the witness, and a bag of coke tucked in my dress sleeve. Anyway, like I said, I asked for my papers to be drawn up while I had the courage to do it.

The counselors, (you know who you are), were great. They were supportive, understanding, caring, and firm. The step I made that day was one of the scariest, invigorating, and greatest I did in my life. I knew I wanted out of this way of life and I had to be serious about this decision because if not I would be swept back in easily.

There are so many things that go through your mind when you make a decision to change the very thing you lived for and loved.

There are so many questions that you ask yourself and that a lot of people fail to tell you when they share their story of getting out of any type of abuse or/and addiction.

How will I make it with all these kids?

Where are we going to live?

Who would want me with so many kids?

What about all the issues I have and am dealing with?

Who's going to help me?

Now, I was on my own with four little boys looking at me, "like now what?" And I was looking at them like," I don't know!"

The stay at the battered woman shelter was only for a short time and I had to find a place for us to go. So we went from shelter to shelter with days of having to leave at 8 in the morning and not being allowed back in until after 4 pm.

We had to go out in the winter with snow on the ground and nowhere to go. So we made the best of it at the local library.

It was too cold to walk to my mom's house and some days she refused to come get us.

I finally got a job at the local coffee shop where I made good tips and they took good care of my sons when I brought them there.

We stayed at a local shelter where churches came through to minister to the people who lived there.

I was already going to a local church nearby but I didn't want to be left in the shelter on or right before Thanksgiving. So I signed up to go to another church on those other open days.

I will never forget that particular time because I met some of the most giving people I have met in a long time.

The church was in Bear, Delaware. So one of the ladies picked us up and we were greeted by the congregation with opened arms and good food. They kept in touch with us for a very long time after we left the shelter. They helped us with security deposit for my little apartment, school clothes for the boys, and interview clothes for me.

I will be forever grateful for all they have done for my sons and me.

Do you remember a date in your LIFE when you made a choice to stop something or remove yourself from a situation or circumstance? _____

So, the sun **DID NOT** spring up and the birds **DID NOT** start chirping as soon as I left my husband and the abuse.

Just as I said it wasn't easy for us after we made the decision to leave that abusive relationship. I made a lot of bad decisions after leaving because I didn't know what to do with myself or these very active boys.

I went in and out of relationships and marriages because I was too afraid to be alone with myself and grabbing anyone to be a father figure for my boys, not knowing that I was making matters worse instead of better for them.

The stuff they went through with me as I dealt with these people looking back was really bad.

But, these are the things people don't want to tell when they talk about their life of coming out of situations or circumstances.

Most of the time, it takes a long time and effort along with a lot of bumps, bruises, mistakes and honesty before you come to the place of normalcy.

I look at my sons, who are now grown, and wonder if I had more positive influences in their lives, how far would they be with their talents.

First of all, Single parenting is/was not easy.

Secondly, I was too young to know who I was AND raise four boys.

So that journey definitely didn't start out right.

Oh my God! I'm all alone!

What am I going to do?

I know that a lot of books have been written about coming out and going through but I want to get to the root of the problem!

Where did it come from?

Nine times out of ten it started somewhere in your **childhood!**

It's self-esteem issues!

It's abandonment issues!

Always being picked on

Not having that parent around to cover you like you needed

Some kind of molestation happened in your life.

Some kind of trauma

GO BACK AND FIND OUT WHERE IT CAME FROM! YOU HAVE TO FACE THAT FIRST BEFORE YOU CAN GET COMPLETELY HEALED.

THIS IS YOUR MOMENT TO FACE THE FIRE AND TO EXSTINGUISH THE FIRE! LET ME REMIND YOU AGAIN! YOU ARE NOT IN THIS ALONE!

Let me say this, *THE DEVIL IS SHREWD IN WHAT HE DOES!*

When he got a glimpse into your future and saw the promises that God had for you, his plan to DESTROY YOU started at the very moment that you were conceived!

So, it is vital to make sure that once you have the information about the ENEMY and his plan for your life, you guard yourself by any means necessary!

Trust me. That is easier said than done!

This is when the scriptures stand up and take precedence over everything else. *This* is one of the reasons why you have to get into your Word (Bible) and know it for yourself.

So when the attacks come, you can start fighting back because **FOR REAL** the Devil only backs down when the **Word of God** fight him back.

Now these are just examples of what we have to do when the fight is raging.

When the attack on your mind comes, you will fight with the word of God.

"YOU WILL KEEP HIM IN PERFECT PEACE, WHOSE MIND IS STAYED ON YOU, BECAUSE HE TRUSTS YOU." Isaiah 26:3.

This is done with Worship to inundate yourself with constant reminders of WHO God is to you and How HE has been there for you. Think of those things which are good, holy, of a good report, of victory, of protection, of provision and of LOVE.

If we feel the world, family, job, or anything else is against us, then we go to the Word and fight saying, "If God is for us, who can be against us!" Romans 8:31.

Understand that God is our GOOD FATHER! He will protect and guard HIS child!

Yes, I said we, because it still is a constant reminder that this is an ongoing battle to remember what we need to do to stay FOCUSED.

Now there are some things that need to be uncovered.

I can tell you, "because you are saved, the world is a bed of roses!" and that would be a LIE BECAUSE IT'S NOT TRUE! News flash! When you change sides ALL HELL BREAKS LOOSE!

The very things that didn't bother you and the people you thought were your friends, all of that changes.

Habits that you didn't mind having and things you didn't mind doing start to be strange or bad to you.

The Bible says, *"that the older or season women and men of God should teach the younger or new babes in Christ so that you will know what is happening and why it's happening to you or in your life." Titus 2:1-15*

If (we) held true to those verses some of the falling away in the church would not be happening because the Word of God would back up the instructions that were given.

I have to let things be known so that we can be better in the things of God and advance in the building of the Kingdom of God.

My life has been an example so that we can take the mistakes and lessons as a growing experience that God can use anything and make the best out of a mess.

I never would think to be this far in God to write it down on paper or that it would even matter to anyone but that shows our plans are not His plans.

I had to grasp the fact that I would have to come up with a title and material that would be interesting to read.

Did you read what I said?

I said, "**I would have to come up with.**"

No, through prayer and meditation God was going to inspire everything I needed to fulfill whatever assignment He had for me.

So I sat down and began to go over my life this far and it all started flowing.

There are people who need to hear that you can make it out of an abusive relationship with your life and can start over successfully.

Think about a prior or current relationship that you have had with a loved one. How did it play a part in the shaping of your life? Is/Was it beneficial to your growth? Is/Was it healthy?

_____

_____

_____

_____

_____

_____

_____

_____

_____

_____

_____

_____

Fire Starter

There are drug addicts that need to know that it does not always have to be jail, AA, NA or the grave to make you stop and never pick up again.

There is a single parent, who's at wits end, with the children and don't know where the next meal is coming from who needs to know that **IT WILL BE ALRIGHT.**

I'm praying for you.

I hope that even if that particular person does not read this book, someone that they are connected to who has read this book can give them the advice or the encouragement from what they have read.

CAN YOU DO THAT? WILL YOU DO THAT?

This change didn't come over night. Matter of fact, it actually took many years to come to the place and self-esteem that I may be able to really write something worth reading.

When I say worth reading, I'm talking about one of those kinds of books that you can quote a phrase when talking to someone.

So AGAIN, the sun didn't spring up and the birds didn't start chirping as soon as I left my husband and the abuse.

MAN LOOK! When I left their dad it was August 13,1993 and I can truly say that it has taken more than 10 years before I could get my head on *half-way* straight.

There is no hand book in the world that would or will be able to prepare you for the life changes and obstacles you go through *except* the Bible.

You will face things about your family, your friends, your children and yourself that will help determine if you are a SURVIVOR.

What I found out through my own experience, is that when you come out of something negative that has been holding you for a long time, it seems like the people around you are the biggest doubters.

I don't know if it's on purpose or if it's subconsciously done.

I just know they are not the greatest support all the time.

So when you realize that this may be a road that you may have to walk alone then you will make the proper adjustments to do what you have to do to walk through it..

I will tell you that your relationship with God will become extremely intimate. **Why?** You ask?

There will be nights that you will cry out to Him to make the pain go away or for the experience to hurry up and be over.

The intimacy between you and your Savior will be so open where you will ask questions that you have probably been wanting to ask for a very long time but didn't know how or thought it might be disrespectful.

The levels of closeness between the creature and Creator will become so trusted that the communication will be one that flows.

This is not an easy place to be in because the loneliness is real and the isolation is, too.

Again, I tell you to build your prayer life and a circle of people who will pray for you in your time of transition and that God hears and they can hear Him too.

If you don't have a place of worship or sanctuary to call home, get one! This is not an easy place and you will need all the help you can get.

*Can you find or do you have a church home now?*_____

*Do have anyone you know that has a trusting prayer life (someone who's life is committed to prayer and it's effective?)*_____

If the answer is YES, then connect with them in this process.

If the answer is NO, ask the True and Living God in the name of Jesus to send someone pure in Spirit to pray with and for you in this process.

Jesus, when He was in the Garden of Gethsemane (**Luke 22:39-46**), even asked if the task of the Cross could pass from Him.

He was afraid! He was alone because the people He had brought with Him were asleep! He was human for that moment! Why? So He could feel the feelings we have and be able to understand them.

That's why the word says, *"HE WAS TOUCHED WITH OUR INFIRMITIES (Hebrews 4:15)."*

Life through the FIRE is not easy!

I found and yet am finding that there are old habits, mind-sets, mannerisms, vocabularies, dispositions, attitudes, enemies that need to be destroyed.

We believe and respond to what concerns us the most.

What affects our life and our world is where we focus our attention.

It is usually through some transition or tragedy that demands us to take notice of what is really going on for us to decide to take action.

There are certain trials and tribulations that will make you... make the choice to take the stand for your life, your children, your future, and your destiny.

Is there anything you can think of right now that has you concerned?

Do you think you are taking the correct stand for that thing which is giving you concern ? Why or Why not?

This is the FIRE PROCESS!!

This is the process where you get put into the FIRE and the impurities that you have acquired are being burned out and off of you.

You find out that just like being burned by the oven, stove or hot water, it HURTS!!!!

It hurts your feelings, attitude, thinking, dialogue, and most of all, your LIFE!!!!

It's like being put in the furnace and after you have been in a situation for awhile you are taken out.

Or while you're in the Fire the heat is turned up to go deeper and get those hidden impurities like PRIDE, SELF PITY, LOW SELF-ESTEEM, UNFORGIVENESS and HEART HURTS.

No one can put a time or a limit on how long it will take for this process to end but God and you.

I say you because you can decide how long it takes for you to accept the plans of God and to follow the directions He gave you.

Some experiences you will repeat! Honestly speaking!

Question... Is there something that you KNOW you have stopped that you are supposed to be doing, handling or confronting right NOW?

WHAT IS IT?

_____

_____

_____

_____

_____

_____

_____

_____

_____

_____

_____

You will repeat these experiences because some of them are ways of the Fire.

It's what I was talking about earlier because there are still impurities that have to come out.

Will you be upset about it? YES!

Will you oppose the process? YES!

Will you feel it is not fair or stupid? YES!

WILL IT STOP? NO!

Well, no that's not true.

It can stop or be aborted if you jump out of the Fire and stop the process.

There is no easy way to put it but it will definitely be worth it all.

You will make mistakes because you are human but you forgive yourself and others quickly then keep moving forward.

Stay honest with God, yourself and others by any means and all means necessary.

Work on You!!!

What can you do to work on YOU?

_____

_____

_____

_____

_____

Loving you!

What can YOU do to Love You?

_____

_____

_____

_____

_____

Caring for you!

What can you do to care for yourself?

_____

_____

_____

_____

_____

Accepting you!

What is it about yourself that you have to ACCEPT?

_____

_____

_____

_____

_____

Providing for you!

Where have YOU fallen short providing for yourself?

_____

_____

_____

_____

_____

and enjoying you!

What can YOU do to enjoy YOU?

_____

_____

_____

_____

_____

Most of all getting to KNOW YOU!!!

How WELL do you know YOU?

_____

_____

_____

_____

_____

Understand this...

The Fire Process... will burn off the lies that have been told to you by others and yourself.

The Fire Process... will burn off the insecurities that have been embedded into your consciousness.

The Fire Process... will burn the secret pains that have been embedded in your being.

And I will put this third into the fire, and refine them as one refines silver, and test them as gold is tested. They will call upon my name, and I will answer them. I will say, 'They are my people'; and they will say, 'The Lord is my God.'" Zechariah 13:9

Think about that for a minute.

What are you willing to undergo to get to the Promises of God?

So even the Bible gives US heads up about the pressure and the test that WE have to go through by saying, HE will put US in the Fire and REFINE US and then TEST US. WAIT!WHAT???

I had to look up what these words meant – fire, refine, and test – because my sister, Charee said, "we assume we know the meaning of a word and really we don't have the FULL definition of that particular word.

FIRE – a controlled occurrence of fire created by burning something in a special area (such as a fireplace or stove); a destructive burning. (Merriam-Webster Dictionary)

REFINE – to free from impurities or unwanted material: to free from moral imperfection: to improve or perfect by pruning or polishing: to reduce in vigor or intensity: to free from what is coarse, vulgar, or uncouth: to become pure or perfected.

TEST – a critical examination, observation, or evaluation: a basis for evaluation:

So the thought of God putting us in the Fire to activate the burning away or to surface the crap we had or have in us makes our jaws drop in disbelief that He would actually do that to us.

I remember I did not have a car and I had the boys and we were trying to get on the bus but I refused to ask for help. I mean REFUSED!!!!

The boys were the ages from 4 to 1, a double stroller, and a diaper bag and I would not ask or accept help!!!

What was my problem?

I had it in my mind that I would never ask anybody for help or accept help because THEY want something in return.

So, with that mindset, it got very hard for me because there were times when I missed the bus, missed my stop, or ended up hurting myself trying do everything by myself instead of asking for help.

Now, the heat (*fire*) of the situation was going to continue or intensify with missing buses, missing stops, and hurting myself until the confronting and removing (**refining**) of **pride, rejection, and guilt** took place. This was not an easy process just because I did not want to let it go.

I did not want to rely on anybody else to help me with my children, my responsibilities, or my stuff!

The thought of being looked at as helpless or a statistic was something I could not tolerate, even though inside, I felt like I was another statistic. It was not easy and it was not until I let go of the stinking thinking I had that it seemed that things started to change.

I had help with my change of thought by accepting the invitation to go to a church from some ladies canvassing the area as part of outreach for a local church.

I accepted the invitation and I can say that was when my life started changing for the better.

Again, it was not over night or a miracle sensation but rededicating my life to God sure did make a difference.

I definitely was in the Fire process and it was not pleasant because you have to deal with you, the REAL you.

The Real you is the part that has to be Refined and molded and cut and then sometimes placed back into the Fire.

No, don't put the book down now and shake your head talking about, "man, ain't nobody doing all of that!"

My question would be why not?

Are you not worth it?

It is very uncomfortable having to go against what you've always thought about yourself or what others had said to you and you believed.

So, that is why we have to be able to stay and endure the heat of the FIRE process but if we can endure the FIRE process it will be worth it.

The process will be WORTH IT! I promise you, beloved, it will be WORTH IT!

The hardest part of the process is to believe that all the things you may have to face is going to somehow come together to work for your GOOD.

Here is the PROMISE...

In the book of **Romans 8:28** *"And we know that all things work together for good to them that love God, to them who are the called according to his purpose."*

From beginning to end, all of our encounters will work together to bring us to a REAL PUROSE, a REAL GLORIOUS OUTCOME, and a REAL DESTINY!

<u>The Fire process cannot be and is not for everyone!</u>

Everyone cannot and will not come with you to and through the Fire process! You may want your sister, your mother, your husband or your best friend to come, but none of them can come with you through the process.

The FIRE process is for you and not anyone else this time.

We are so used to grasping for people around as to help us through our process but not this time!

This is YOUR PROCESS!

It is going in the Fire process that WE come out as pure Gold! We are made to endure, to understand, to comprehend, to trust, to believe and to, most of all, GLORIFY our God!

I had to go through the Fire process over and over and over again and will go through the Fire process until the day God calls me home to Heaven!

The Fire process never stops but it is easier when we yield to it and trust that God knows exactly what He is doing.

I am daily looking at my Life and seeing how I have to go back into prayer sometimes because that habit, thought or attitude has not died and that shows me that my process is not over, not by a long shot.

We don't make excuses for sin or short-comings. We recognize them and deal with them immediately! It is that transformed mindset that you have to keep to stay VICTORIOUS over the flesh.

We have to remember that the Word of God says, *"The Spirit is willing but the flesh is weak." Matt. 26:41*

This is our constant reminder that we cannot make excuses but we can dive into our secret place with God and let Him do it! Let God put us in the FIRE so we can shine like the Gold He has intended for us to be.

He had our lives mapped out from the beginning of time.

All the rough and uncomfortable areas of our lives will work together, if we love Him enough, trust His Word and the leading of the Holy Spirit.

We have to continue to be willing and open to the molding and shaping of our being so that we can be everything that God has called us to be.

There will always be days of discouragement or disappointment because that is the human part of us.

There are days when we will not feel all the lovely things we have been told by God or see all the promises He has told us either. But we have to keep the faith to know what God said will be.

There will be hardships that are going to come to make us question what in the world is going on and if God is paying attention to what we are going through.

Lo and behold, we will eventually find out that God is paying more attention to us than we thought.

So, regardless of how *we* feel, God thinks nothing like we think and again, His ways are definitely not our ways.

He takes us daily through the obstacles and situations of Life to bring us to the good and expected end that He has promised us in His Word.

We do not have to believe the lies of the enemy concerning our lives.

Mistakes are made by everyone in the world and it is what you do with your mistakes that determines where you are going.

I had to shake myself, just like the prodigal son did. Read Luke 15:11-32:

"The young man finally comes to his senses, remembering his father. In humility, he recognizes his foolishness, decides to return to his father and ask for <u>forgiveness</u> *and mercy. The father who had been watching and waiting, receives his son back with open arms of compassion. He is* <u>overjoyed</u> *by the return of his lost son! Immediately the father turns to his servants and asks them to prepare a giant feast in celebration."*

That's how God views us!

Like I said I had to come to my senses and stop waddling in my mess and sin and get up and come home back to God!

Abuse strips you of so much and so many things in your life that you have to literally rebuild and remind yourself that you are an Over-comer and Victorious.

Consuming Fire

Now becoming Victorious and an Over-comer is a mindset of sacrifice because you have come to the place that you know that you cannot do it by yourself.

You also have come to the place that regardless of how bad it looks and even gets, sometimes you serve a God that know where you are and is concerned about YOU.

When you have realized where you are you will know that you are in the presence of the Consuming Fire of the Holy Spirit.

This is the leading into all Truth, Understanding, Commitment, and most of all, Love again.

This Consuming Fire will burn up all the doubt you have concerning a matter if you let Him.

We don't see Him but we can see His Love in everything around us and it's in that Love that our hang-ups are CONSUMED by the Fire of His Love.

When you are in the place of God's consuming, Love it is just that CONSUMING!!

That means that He will continually come and cover places of your life not touchable or was not reachable because it was covered with hurt, pain, fear, rejection, and/or anger.

God knows all of that and is willing to come down to where we are and ENGULF/CONSUME us.

We then have to acknowledge Him working in our lives.

Consuming Fire means to invade that very thing that is present in our life and take it over so that it is completely taken over, endowed, overwhelmed, and changed by the Fire that has come to burn up the sin, restraints, obstacles and hindrances in our life. To be consumed by the ways of God is a complete yielding of our ways of thinking, reacting and responding to things in our lives and how we work out the kinks that come.

God knows that this is not an easy overnight sensation but it is doable. I have had to separate myself from the very people I loved to become and yet becoming who God has called me to be in this life.

It doesn't matter where, when, and how you started but it matters how YOU end!

So with that being said, this is how I'm going to end this 1st book........

You are not alone and you CAN and WILL make it! How BAD DO YOU WANT YOUR LIFE TO BEGIN AGAIN? IT STARTS WITH YOU! I LOVE YOU AND WILL TALK TO YOU SOON!!

NOTES TO AND FOR YOURSELF

_____

_____

_____

_____

_____

_____

_____

_____

_____

_____

GOOD JOB!!!

Our Prayer

Father God, in the name of Jesus, I pray
for everyone that read this book.

Lord, I pray that they find the direction,
guidance and understanding that they need to
go to the next level in their life and to know that
there is LIFE AFTER (*fill in the blanks)!*

God, I pray that you heal the broken pieces
of our life and touch men, women, girls,
boys and people of all walks of life.

God, I pray that as they remember the things that they
read, they should know that they are not alone and that
you care for them and most of all LOVE THEM.

We bind every spirit of the enemy that has come
to cause anyone who has read this book to feel less
than Wonderfully made, Intelligent, Able to change
and to OVER-COME ANY OBSTACLE AND BE
VICTORIOUS. THANK YOU GOD FOR THE LIFE
CHANGING EVENTS AND PRAISE REPORTS THAT
ARE TO COME AFTER THIS!!! IN JESUS' LIFE
CHANGING NAME!!!!!

AMEN

Email me: tarareeves730@gmail.com

FaceBook: Tara Reeves

Youtube: iLivefitb...Tara Reeves

www.ingramcontent.com/pod-product-compliance
Lightning Source LLC
Chambersburg PA
CBHW020732250626
47155CB00006B/2258

* 9 780999 159019 *